For my brothers, Mick, Skip, Terry, and Tommie,
who made every day a holiday –Pegi

For my parents, Frances *and* Stephen Weill –Cindy

Thanks to Nguyễn Ngọc Hương, Dan Rocovits,
Anne Sippel, Jenna *and* Jack Foley, Dave *and*
Diane Young, Chris Gilson, Ellen K. Dry,
Bùi Thị Ngọc Bích, Jack Bailey, Hữu Ngọc,
Đỗ Thanh Hương, Anabel Jackson,
Nguyễn Bích Thuỷ, Nguyễn Diệu Anh,
Nguyễn Thị Lệ Khanh, Hoàng Thu Hương,
Christy Trinh, *and* Suzanne Lecht.

Very special thanks to Wendy *and* Chris Gibbs,
Jean *and* Stefan Golicz, Đặng Văn Bài, *and*
Thái Thị Hạnh Nhân.

Text © 2003 by Pegi Deitz Shea.
Illustrations © 2003 by Cynthia Weill.

Book design by Eun Young Lee and Kristine Brogno.
Typeset in Catull and Bell Gothic.
The illustrations in this book were embroidered in cotton thread.
Manufactured in Hong Kong.

Library of Congress Cataloging-in-Publication Data
Shea, Pegi Deitz.
Ten mice for Tet / Pegi Deitz Shea and Cynthia Weill.
p. cm.
Summary: A village of mice prepares for Tet, or Vietnamese
New Year, as different numbers of mice give gifts, cook
food, and celebrate in other traditional ways. Includes an
afterword with facts about the holiday.
ISBN 0-8118-3496-4
1. Vietnamese New Year–Juvenile literature. 2. Vietnam–Social
life and customs–Juvenile literature. [1. Vietnamese New Year.
2. Vietnam–Social life and customs. 3. Holidays. 4. Counting.]
I. Weill, Cynthia II. Title.
GT4905 .S44 2003
394.2614–dc21
2002007456

Distributed in Canada by Raincoast Books
9050 Shaughnessy Street, Vancouver, British Columbia V6P 6E5

10 9 8 7 6 5 4 3 2 1

Chronicle Books LLC
85 Second Street, San Francisco, California 94105

www.chroniclekids.com

Ten Mice for Tet

By **Pegi Deitz Shea** *and* **Cynthia Weill**

Illustrations by **Tô Ngọc Trang**

Embroidery by **Phạm Viết Đinh**

chronicle books san francisco

It's time for Tet!

1 mouse plans a party.

2 mice go to market.

3 mice paint and polish.

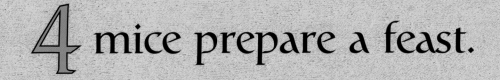
4 mice prepare a feast.

5 mice learn their fortunes.

6 mice open presents.

7 mice dance and play.

8 mice make music.

9 mice eat Tet treats.

10 mice watch fireworks.

Happy New Year!
Chúc Mừng Năm Mới!

About Tet

Tết Nguyên Đàn (pronounced Tet Nyen Don) is the celebration of the new year in Vietnam. It means "Feast of the First Day," and Tet, as it's called for short, begins on the first day of the lunar calendar. To the Vietnamese, it is as big a celebration as Easter, Thanksgiving, and Christmas combined! In addition to the traditional Tet celebrations, weddings are often held around the holiday season, because the harvest has finished and the people take time off from work.

Tet takes place over four days at the end of January and the beginning of February on the Western calendar. It unites ancestors of the past; family and friends of the present, who may travel home to celebrate together; and hopes and dreams for the future. Tet also unites the household genies: the Kitchen God, the Craft God, and the Land God. Each new year in a twelve-year cycle is named after a different animal in order: Rat, Buffalo, Tiger, Cat, Dragon, Snake, Horse, Goat, Monkey, Rooster, Dog, Pig.

As with any language, the pronunciation of Vietnamese words can vary from region to region. However, in an attempt to help the reader pronounce the Vietnamese words in these pages an approximate phonetic spelling of each word follows it in parentheses.

1 mouse plans a party.

A successful Tet celebration promises good luck for the next twelve months. That's why everyone works so hard to prepare. Debts are paid, lists are written, duties are assigned, and guests are invited. A Vietnamese family visits with the family of their father on the first day of Tet and the family of their mother on the second day. On the third day, friends celebrate together in a home or outdoors. The Vietnamese "invite" their ancestors to their Tet celebrations by burning incense and offering food at an altar, and they send greeting cards to loved ones near and far.

2 mice go to market.

Among the many things the Vietnamese buy for Tet are lamp oil, incense, salt, ingredients for special snacks and meals, and flowers and plants for decoration. Flowers have important meanings. For example, the narcissus brings success and prosperity. And the more apricot and peach flowers the Vietnamese have blooming on the first day of Tet, the more happiness they will receive in the coming year.

3 mice paint and polish.

All over the world, people make their homes clean and beautiful for special holidays. The Vietnamese are no different. In addition to cleaning and decorating, they welcome good spirits and chase away devils by "planting" a *Neû* (neo), a decorated bamboo pole, and offering a *mâm ngũ quả* (mum noo qua), "five-fruit tray," at the family altar. They make themselves beautiful, too, with new clothes and fragrances.

4 mice prepare a feast.

Families prepare an abundance of food to serve to guests. Popular dishes include pickled vegetables, meat pies or meat stewed in coconut milk, and *mứt* (mut)—candied fruits and jams. The most traditional Tet food is the *bánh chưng* (ban chun), a rice cake stuffed with pork, spices, and bean paste. Legend has it that the recipe came to a prince in a dream thousands of years ago. Wrapped and cooked in banana leaves, the *bánh chưng* contains only healthy ingredients to protect the body.

5 mice learn their fortunes.

Fortune-tellers are very busy before and during Tet. They read palms and predict whether a person will have good or bad luck, marry, divorce, or have children. The Vietnamese hope that all their preparation for Tet will result in only good fortune. The Vietnamese also hang *câu đối* (ko doy), "parallels," red banners with written wishes for intelligence, morality, and well being for everyone. The color red stands for happiness and luck. And on the eve of Tet, people pray to the Twelve Highnesses in Heaven who control the earth. The Vietnamese blend folk beliefs like this with the more formal religions of Confucianism, Taoism, and Buddhism.

6 mice open presents.

Vietnamese children do not receive gifts on their birthdays. But they do receive them on Tet! The most common gift is *lì xì* (lee cee), new money notes tucked inside a red embossed envelope. Visitors also bring presents of cookies, tea, fruit, and other delicacies. The *người khách đầu tiên* (newy kak dow tien), "first visitor," on Tet must be a lucky one who brings gifts.

7 mice dance and play.

On the third day of Tet, the Vietnamese celebrate outdoors, nibbling on barbecued meat sticks, singing traditional songs, performing the lion or dragon dance, watching puppet shows, visiting a temple or pagoda, and reciting poetry. They play games, such as human chess and tug-of-war, and compete in sports, such as running and wrestling.

8 mice make music.

The Vietnamese play many instruments. They include the *kèn* (ken), a pan-flute; the *đàn tam thập lục* (don tam tap look), a 36-chord zither; the *cồng chiêng* (kong chien), a gong; the *đàn nguyệt* (don wit), a two-stringed guitar; the *T-rưng* (ta run), a bamboo xylophone; the *sáo* (sao), a flute; the *đàn bầu* (don bow), a monochord; and the *trong* (chom), a drum.

9 mice eat Tet treats.

Special Tet treats include *xôi gấc* (soy guk), sticky rice flavored with a red fruit; *mứt gừng* (mut gung), candied ginger; *mứt dừa* (mut zua), sugar-coated coconut; and *hạt dưa rang* (hat zua rang), roasted melon seeds.

10 mice watch fireworks.

It's traditionally believed that the crackling of firecracker strings scares away evil for the coming year. Villages, towns, and cities have huge, colorful firework displays, which fill the skies with blooms of light.

Happy New Year! Chúc Mừng Năm Mới!

Many of Vietnam's fifty-four minority groups have their own language or dialect, but everyone knows that *Chúc Mừng Năm Mới!* (Chuk Mung Nam Moi) means "Happy New Year!"